Shaun the Sheep™
Abracadabra
and
Save the Tree

EGMONT

We bring stories to life

First Published in Great Britain 2008 by Egmont UK Limited. 239 Kensington High Street, London W8 6SA

© and ™ Aardman Animations Ltd. 2008. All rights reserved.
Shaun the Sheep (word mark) and the character 'Shaun the Sheep' © and ™ Aardman Animations Limited.
Based on a character created by Nick Park. Developed by Richard (Golly) Goleszowski with Alison Snowden and David Fine.
ISBN 978 1 4052 4167 0
1 3 5 7 9 10 8 6 4 2
Printed in Singapore

Abracadabra

One morning, Bitzer was standing beside the farmhouse door, wondering what on earth his master could be doing.

Inside, the Farmer was grunting and humphing to himself. Every now and then, a tin can flew out of the door towards the recycling tubs and landed with a clang! Bitzer tried to catch the cans and balance them on the overflowing boxes.

Bitzer realised the Farmer was clearing out his kitchen.

Shaun came up to see what all the noise was about. As he approached the farmhouse, a pair of grotty old underpants came flying out and landed on his head!

Shaun shook the pants off and snorted.

grunt!

Inside the kitchen, the Farmer had thrown out most of the empty cans, along with a broken teapot and a Rubik's cube. He growled grumpily to himself. How had he managed to collect so much rubbish?

Then he spotted something at the back of the cupboard. It was an old box of magic tricks.

"Ah!" he exclaimed.

The Farmer pulled out the box and smiled. Magic tricks would be just the thing for the next time his niece came to visit!

Meanwhile, Shaun and Bitzer were peering in through the kitchen window. They were glad the Farmer had stopped throwing smelly rubbish at them, but they wondered what he was going to do with the shabby old box.

The Farmer put the box on the table and opened it up. There were lots of brightly coloured things inside, but the Farmer picked up a black stick with a white tip at each end. It was a magic wand!

The Farmer shook the wand, hoping that wonderful magic would suddenly happen. Instead, the stick sagged in the middle like a dead plant.

Shaun began to snigger, tee hee hee! Bitzer had to get him to shut up.

The Farmer frowned and shook the wand again. Flowers burst from the tip.

tee hee hee!

"Oooh!" exclaimed the Farmer. That was more like it!

Now he wanted to try more tricks.

The Farmer took a blue tube covered with stars out of the box and tapped it with the wand. There was a ping, and when he lifted up the tube, an empty bottle had been magicked into the space underneath it!

This was fun! The Farmer smiled again.

But he didn't smile for long. Every time he put down the tube, it made another bottle — then another, and another! Soon the Farmer's table was covered with useless bottles.

"Aarrghh!" yelled the Farmer, losing his temper. As if he hadn't got enough rubbish already!

He picked up the box of magic tricks and threw it out of the door. But it didn't land in the bin. Shaun caught it, and rushed off to the barn to show the flock.

"Grrr!" growled Bitzer, running after Shaun. The naughty sheep was bound to get up to mischief with a box of magic tricks!

But when Bitzer reached the barn, he was so impressed by Shaun's tricks that he soon forgot to be annoyed. The little sheep had found a top hat in the magic box, and was pulling a great big lampshade out of it.

Ooooh!

Bitzer took the lamp, stand and all and **thumped** it down on the barn floor. Then he remembered what he was supposed to be doing and started scolding Shaun again.

But Shaun wasn't bothered by Bitzer. He tapped the hat with the wand again. This time a bird came out, **squawked** loudly and flew up to sit in the rafters of the barn.

thump!

The sheep all sat down to watch the show. They thought Shaun's latest trick was very clever — especially when the bird did a poo on Bitzer's head!

Bitzer didn't think it was funny at all. He got out a handkerchief and wiped his forehead. But while the sheepdog's back was turned, Shaun climbed into the top hat.

When Bitzer had cleaned his face, he was ready to give Shaun a telling-off. But the sneaky sheep vanished!

The flock looked around, waiting to see what would happen. Then the old wardrobe that stood in the corner of the barn began to creak and rattle.

creak

ping!

Bitzer strode over and pulled open the door. Out came Shaun, covered in dust, and still holding the wand.

Shaun waved the wand again, and with a ping Bitzer vanished! All the sheep gasped. Another wave of the wand, and Bitzer was back. But there was something very unusual about him. In place of his dog collar, a ring of huge pink petals surrounded his neck! Bitzer's face looked out from the middle, very surprised.

Baa ha ha!

"Huh?" Bitzer whimpered.

All the sheep pointed at him, and fell about laughing, Baaa ha ha!

Every time Shaun pointed the wand at Bitzer, something even sillier happened.

First the petals around his neck moved down his body to make him a lovely pink skirt. Next, a big red clown's nose appeared on his face. Then his ears sprouted purple fluffy feathers!

Finally Bitzer disappeared again. But just at that moment, the flock froze. The Farmer was whistling outside in the field.

Bitzer had to go to his master, even though he was invisible!

Out in the field, the Farmer was looking for his dog. He got a big shock when the gate creaked open, but nobody was there!

ahhhhhh!

Shaun heard the Farmer coming and quickly magicked all the sheep invisible. When the Farmer looked into the barn, he was very puzzled to see it empty. Then he stepped back — and trod on his dog.

"Yooowww!" wailed the invisible Bitzer.

"Aaarrrggh!" cried the Farmer. He ran straight back to the farmhouse and lay down with a bag of ice cubes on his head. He thought he must be ill, and this would make him feel better.

chomp!

Meanwhile, Shaun magicked everyone back again. The next time the Farmer looked out of his window, he saw Bitzer counting the sheep as normal.

"Phew!" he said.

But Shaun was worried. Shirley was nowhere to be seen. And there were chomping sounds coming from the farmhouse kitchen!

buuurp!

Shaun and Bitzer crept into the kitchen. They could hear **slurping** and **gulping**. A huge cake seemed to be floating in mid-air. As they watched, a chunk of the cake disappeared. Then another, and another!

Shaun knew what must be happening. He waved his wand and, with a giant **buuurp**, Shirley appeared.

The Farmer heard the burp, too! He jumped out of bed and came hurrying downstairs, waving a big wooden brush. He thought there were burglars in his kitchen, and he was ready to chase them off! So he was relieved when he found Shirley and Shaun instead of robbers.

Bitzer pretended that he had just found the sheep scoffing the Farmer's cake, and was telling them off. His master patted him on the head for being a good dog.

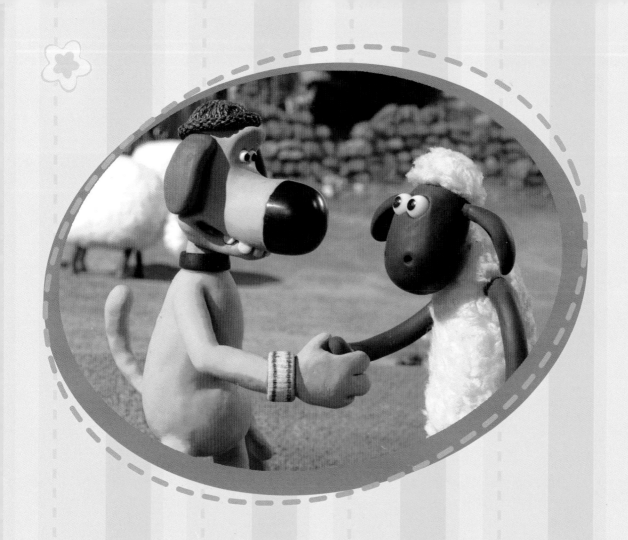

Shirley stared at the rest of the lovely cake and sighed. She had so wanted to finish it! But she and Shaun had to trot obediently out of the kitchen.

Outside in the sunshine, Shaun shook Bitzer's paw. They made a good team. Bitzer had stopped the Farmer from finding out that the sheep had been using his wand. In return, Shaun had made Bitzer look good in front of his master by trotting meekly back to the field.

Even Shirley did not stay sad for long, because the sheep got the last laugh. Shaun had not undone all the magic spells.

When Bitzer turned to walk across the field, everyone could see what had happened to his bottom, and they all sniggered. Everyone, that was, except Bitzer himself. He still had a big pink flower growing out of his tail!

hee-hee-hee!

Save the Tree

One morning, the Farmer woke up shivering. It was absolutely freezing in his bedroom! His breath made a cloud in the air, his teeth chattered like maracas and the glass of water by his bed had turned to ice. Brrrrr!

Really, it was lucky he hadn't remembered to take his teeth out the night before and put them in the glass, but the Farmer was too cold to be glad about that.

Then he realised what the problem was. The wood fire that should have been burning warmly had fizzled out overnight. Now it was just a pile of ash, with a few sad spirals of smoke drifting up the chimney.

Brrrrr!

The Farmer got up and gave the fire a good poke, but it was no use. He needed more wood.

Dressed in his warmest clothes, he went outside to the log store and peered inside. It was almost totally empty! One little twig lay alone at the bottom.

The Farmer let the lid of the bin fall with a clunk.

27

It was time for a trip out in the van to collect some firewood. The Farmer picked up his saw, and whistled for Bitzer. **Phwwweep!**

Over in the field, Bitzer was lifting weights. "**Grrrrr!**" he growled with the effort, but he kept going. If the flock saw him drop a weight on his foot, it could seriously damage his farmyard credibility.

But when the Farmer whistled for him, Bitzer had to go to his master. They loaded the saw into the back of the van, then drove off down the lane.

Three sheep stood staring at the van with innocent expressions on their faces. But as soon as the van was out of sight, the sheep broke into grins and rushed back into their field.

The sheep pushed Shirley up against the base of the big tree so Shaun could use her as a trampoline. Boooiiing! He jumped up into the branches and pulled down the rope swings that were hidden in the branches.

Boooiing!

Soon the sheep were having a swinging time.

Baaaaaaaaaaaaaa!

Some of the flock jumped around in the big tree, while others hung from the branches or swung on the rope swings. Everyone was bleating with excitement. Baaaaaaaaaaaaaa!

One sheep even got an old accordion from the rubbish dump and began playing an Irish jig for her friends to dance to, dum-diddle-dee.

Meanwhile, the Farmer was looking for trees to cut down for firewood. He stopped the van by a group of saplings, but they were all too spindly and pathetic to burn as firewood.

Bitzer knew that bendy young trees don't burn very well, so he pulled one of the saplings to see how flexible it was. It was very bendy indeed – so bendy that it sprang back and hit the Farmer in the face, thwack!

That got Bitzer a telling-off.

thwack!

Finally, the Farmer and Bitzer found a medium-sized tree, and started sawing at it, sKreee! Unfortunately, when it fell, it hit the end of a bench where an old lady was sitting. The old lady flew up in to the air.

The Farmer managed to catch her in his arms, but the old lady was cross and whacked him over the head with her bag. Smack!

sKreee!

Bitzer and the Farmer didn't have much luck with the next tree either. They were so eager to get to it and cut it down that they didn't notice the 'Beware of the dog' sign. A huge, fierce Alsatian chased them away.

Back in the field, the sheep were still having fun in the big tree. They twanged each other off the branches and did bungee jumping with some old elastic rope. One of the sheep got his friends to twist his swing around and around and around.

When they let go the swing span back to normal so fast that the sheep was thrown across the field! BAA – AARGH!

Shaun was at the very top of the tree, keeping watch. When he saw the van coming back, he bleated a warning to the flock. Instantly they pulled up the rope swings. Then they folded up their legs and rolled down from the tree like giant snowballs.

In a few seconds, the field was back to normal. All the sheep were grazing calmly, well away from the big tree.

With a screeeech of brakes, the Farmer halted the van in the lane. His farm looked totally ordinary, but he smiled a wide smile. He had seen just what he was looking for: a nice, big, old, tree. The flock's tree!

Shaun stood watching the Farmer, wondering what was making the old man look so happy. Shaun looked from the van to the tree and back again.

Then the Farmer picked up his saw. Shaun realised with a gasp what was about to happen!

gasp!

Shaun bleated a panic signal to the flock. They all rushed to gather round him and listened to him explain the danger.

What Shaun told them seemed too horrible for his friends to believe. But then they looked at the Farmer with his big, sharp, shiny saw – and they knew the worst was going to happen!

bleat-bleat!

The Farmer grunted with satisfaction at his good idea, and the sheep gasped and trembled. What could the poor woolly-brained animals do against the Farmer and Bitzer?

Shaun had come up with a plan to buy them time. While the Farmer stood admiring the tree and thinking how much lovely firewood it would make, the sheep sneaked into position.

Humph!

When the Farmer started walking towards the tree, he found three big white woolly backsides blocking his path.

"Humph!" he snorted, and stepped to the side. But the sheep edged sideways, staying in front of him.

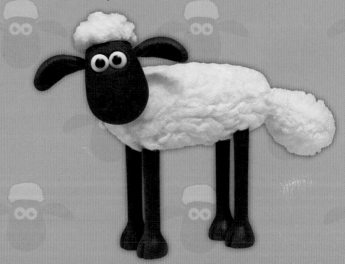

Again the Farmer moved – and again the sheep blocked him.

"Grrarragh!" growled the Farmer. But the flock would not get out of his way.

Finally the Farmer ordered Bitzer to blow his whistle, phweeep! No sheep can disobey that sound. The dog pointed towards their pen, and the three sheep scuttled inside.

phweeep!

rumble

Shaun had a back-up plan. He gave the signal to two of the flock who were waiting on the other side of a stone wall. They had leant an old door against the wall to make a ramp.

Shirley was balanced on top of the wall, with a sweatband under her ears. When Shaun waved, the two sheep gave her a big push, and she rolled down the ramp.

With a ground-shaking rumble, Shirley rolled across the field and hit the Farmer. First he sank into Shirley's fleece and rolled along with her, then she squashed him into the ground, squish!

Shirley hit the far wall with a thump and bounced back to her feet. But the Farmer got up as well, and kept heading for the tree.

AAAAAAARGHH! the Farmer cursed. It was just as well the sheep couldn't understand what he said, because it wasn't very polite!

AAAAAAARGHH!

The sheep still had a few more tricks to try. One of them had dug a hole in front of the tree. The Farmer fell down it, thud! But he just got out again and kept going, even though he was covered in mud.

Soon, Bitzer and the Farmer stood by the big tree, ready to cut it down. But they didn't know what was going on above them.

Shaun and his hand-picked ninja sheep were the last line of defence. They were sitting up in the branches. When the Farmer got too close, they jumped out and pinned him to the ground, thud!

But then Bitzer blew his whistle again. Sheep cannot resist that sound any more easily than your mother can resist wiping your face with a slobbery tissue.

The flock hung their heads and sadly trotted, clomp, clomp, clomp, into their pen.

thud!

gasp!

Again, the Farmer lifted the saw. The horrified sheep could only watch in silence. Not even Shaun could think of anything to do now.

The saw rose **higher!**

The sheep **gasped!**

The Farmer **froze!**

The Farmer said **"Huh?!"**

Then he leant forwards and peered at the trunk of the tree.

He had seen something unexpected. Scratched into the bark was a simple picture of a face.

Suddenly, a memory drifted into the Farmer's mind. He thought back to his childhood, and his memories went black and white, like a boring old film.

The Farmer remembered when he had been a scruffy little boy, running around the farmyard during the school holidays.

chip! chip! chip!

Just like the sheep, he had played in the tree, swinging on the swings and hanging from the branches. He had giggled, tee-hee! as he read comics in the shadow of the branches, and flown his toy plane, wheeeee, around the trunk.

One day he had been especially naughty and borrowed his parents' chisel. With the sharp edge, he had cut a face into the tree's bark, chip! chip! chip!

Now the Farmer stood remembering how happy he had been as a little boy. He went all teary-eyed, like your granny when she looks at old photos. And suddenly he knew: he couldn't possibly cut down this special tree.

The Farmer reached out and hugged the tree, a happy smile on his face. Awwww!

When the sheep saw what had happened, they all grinned. Bitzer got an old bow from the rubbish heap, and used it to play the saw like a violin, scree-eeeeee.

The Farmer stood hugging the tree while Bitzer played and the sun went down behind them.

scree-eeeeee

The tree was saved!